Adventure
in the Night Sky

Adventure
in the Night Sky

Dave Patterson

Illustrated by
Kathy R. Kaulbach

NIMBUS
PUBLISHING

Nimbus Publishing Limited
P.O. Box 9301, Station A
Halifax, N.S.
B3K 5N5

Design Editor: Kathy Kaulbach
Project Editor: Alexa Thompson

Nimbus Publishing Limited gratefully acknowledges the support of the Council of Maritime Premiers and the Department of Communications.

Canadian Cataloguing in Publication Data

Patternson, Dave.

Adventure in the nightsky

(New Waves)

ISBN 0-921054-72-6

I. Kaulbach, Kathy R. (Kathy Rose), 1955-.
II. Title. III. Series.

PS8581.A87A72 1991   jC813'.54   C90-097704-3
Pz7.P37Ad 1991

Printed and bound in Canada

This book is for five girls:
my daughters, Carmen and Charmaine,
and my nieces, Lisa, Sasha and Kelsey—
a generation to watch out for!

Contents

1 Stargazing 1
2 Orion 13
3 On the Run! 28
4 Scorpio 42
5 Pegasus, the Winged Horse 56
6 Cygnus, the Swan......................................69
7 Diana's Revenge 80

1
Stargazing

"Dad, this is so boring!"

Changel squirmed restlessly in her lawn chair and looked at her father. (Her name is pronounced like *angel* with a *ch* in front.) Some of her friends thought her name a little unusual, but her mother and father had chosen it because, they said, "it suited her to a tee."

Changel's chair had been placed in the middle of her family's large backyard, which was on the edge of the little town of Pine Valley on Prince Edward Island. Her father sat nearby in another chair. It was late in the evening—past bedtime.

"Only a few minutes longer, Angel," said her father, peering at the book he was studying by flashlight. The flashlight had a red plastic cover over the bulb to help him read in the dark without interfering with his night vision. "Wasn't it you," he continued, "who thought it would be fun to learn more about some of the stars. Aren't you the one who was excited when you came home from school yesterday?"

The previous day, Dr. Sage, an astronomer, someone who studies the stars, had visited Mrs. Henderson's Grade 5 science class at Pine Valley Elementary School. Changel had been fascinated by her talk, and had told her parents all about it. She had coaxed her father into helping her find a good star book at the library so that they could do some serious star gazing. Now she was beginning to wonder if her idea had been such a good one after all. The night had grown very dark, it was getting cool, and she was feeling very sleepy.

"Dad, maybe we could do this another night. There are millions and millions of stars up there. How can we ever learn about them all?"

Her father turned his head toward her and peered over the top of his wire-rimmed glasses. He smiled at her and she smiled back, although they could hardly see each other in the dark.

"We had better do it tonight, I think," he replied, "while it's still fresh in your mind. It's supposed to cloud over tomorrow for a day or two, and after that there will be a full moon. That means there will be too much light in the sky to see the stars clearly. Besides, I think I have figured it out now. OK?"

"OK, Dad, but can you hurry up, please?" asked Changel, and she leaned back in her chair with a patient sigh. She smothered a big yawn with her hand and looked around the yard.

It was a little spooky this late in the evening. It was after ten o'clock and by this time she was usually snuggled safely in bed under the warm comforter. The house was well behind them; they had seated themselves in the center of the backyard so that the light from the windows wouldn't bother them. Farther down the meadow, where the yard ended, Changel could see the dark branches of the poplar, birch, and maple trees against the sky. The spruce grove that touched the back corner of their lot was black and still. A dark shape flew over it, and the "Whoo-whoo" of the owl, which nested in the wood, echoed through the quiet night.

Changel's eyes grew heavy....

"There now." Changel jumped up from her chair and gave a little squeak. "Hey! Falling asleep on me?" asked her father, grinning.

"Well, maybe," she admitted, trying to sound as though she wasn't.

"No matter," said her father. "Come over here and sit beside me for just a minute or two. I think I've got some of these stars figured out. Maybe you can tell me if I'm right."

"OK, Dad," laughed Changel, and she pulled her chair closer to his. Her father put his arm around her, and she wriggled a little until she rested comfortably against his shoulder.

"Is this what Dr. Sage does when she is not teaching?" she asked. "Does she look at the stars every night?" Her father raised his head from the star book and thought for a moment.

"I suppose so, Angel," he answered, "but I think she probably has a more comfortable chair in a big room with a telescope poking through a hole in the roof. That way she can see the stars more clearly."

"Why a telescope?" asked Changel, "Isn't there enough to see up there without a telescope?"

"There certainly is for me!" replied her father. "Look—there's the constellation called the Big Dipper."

"'Excuse me," interrupted Changel, "the *what* called the big *whatever*?"

"Oh," answered her father, "It's a constellation—a group of stars that appear close to each other in the sky. If you look at them the right way they seem to have a certain shape—of a person or a creature or an object. If you think of them that way, it makes it easier to remember them."

"Right," said Changel. "I know what you mean by the Big Dipper constellation now. Thanks. Dr. Sage did mention it, but I forgot. She also called it by another name, Great Bear, I think."

"Right," said her father. "It seems that astrologers in different places or at different times called the same constellations by different names. Look, the constellation called the Big Dipper, or the Great Bear, is right over there." He pointed toward the north, which was to their left.

"The book says that there are seven stars, four in the shape of a water dipper and three more that make up the handle. That looks like it over there, don't you think?"

Changel looked in the direction of his pointing finger and studied the stars for a moment.

"Yes, I think I see it," she said, concentrating. She pointed with her own finger and counted off the stars in the Big Dipper. "One star in the top corner, then follow an imaginary line down to the second star at the other corner, across to the third star, then back up the opposite way to the fourth—and three more stars for the handle that is bent in the middle."

"Wow, that's great!" she added, her eyes shining in the starlight. "The Big Dipper! It really does look like a water dipper. Mrs. Henderson will be pleased that I found it, or rather *we* found it," she corrected herself quickly.

"Now, look," exclaimed her father, getting almost as excited as Changel, "if we draw an imaginary line through the two stars at the end of the Dipper, straight up—yes—there it is—Polaris. It's that bright star above the Dipper, also called the North Star. Do you see it?"

Changel followed the line he described with her eyes, then nodded. "Polaris," she repeated, "the North Star."

"It says in the book," her father continued, "that Polaris is always in the north, so you can always tell in which direction you are looking. That's how sailors can find their way. That is the first step in navigating by the stars. Well," he finished, "I guess astronomy's not so hard after all."

"Astronomy—one of the oldest sciences," he mused, with a gleam in his eye. Changel had seen that gleam before; it meant that he was getting interested, and that could mean this would turn into an even longer evening.

She yawned, and snuggled deeper into her chair.

"Oh, yes," she said, trying not to give into her drowsiness, "Mrs. Henderson explained that when she introduced us to Dr. Sage. But isn't it almost time to go in? I'm starting to get sleepy."

Her father pulled the collar of jacket up under her chin, and kissed the top of her head.

"You bet, Sweetheart," he said, "but just one more minute. I want to see if I can find one other major constellation. It's called Orion. It's in the shape of a man; you can recognize it by the stars in his belt. There is also a bright star so close to Orion it's called the dog star."

He began to look from the book to the sky, then shone the red light on the book and muttered to himself. He looked at the sky, then back to the book. Changel began to think it was all rather funny. The red light went on … then off … then on … then off … on … off.…

Suddenly the light disappeared. She looked around and noticed a ground fog beginning to creep up through the spruce grove and the trees at the end of the yard. The astronomy book lay closed on her father's lap, and the hand holding the flashlight hung loosely over the side of his lawn chair. His glasses were crooked and his eyes were closed. He breathed deeply, snorted, and then sighed.

"Why, he's falling asleep," thought Changel. She looked at him fondly for a moment, then began to shake him gently.

"Dad, Dad! It's time to go in," she said.

There was no response. She shook him a little harder, and tugged on his shirt sleeve.

She was still shaking him when she realized that the night was growing brighter around her. Then she heard a strange noise behind her and she turned toward it....

"Oh, Dad," she whispered, her eyes growing very wide.

Beside the spruce grove, striding with great, giant steps through the mist was the biggest man imaginable. He must have been at least six metres tall! He looked like the picture of the old Viking that she remembered seeing in one of her school books. He had rippling muscles, long hair and a beard, and the most unusual clothes: an animal skin that stretched over one shoulder and wrapped around his waist, and a skirt that hung down to his knees. He carried a big club in one hand, and a long sword hung from a loop in a wide black belt which circled his waist. He wore sandals on his feet, with laces that criss-crossed up over his calves, almost to his knees. At his side trotted an enormous black dog, its long tongue bouncing wetly from the side of its mouth.

But even stranger than the appearance of this huge pair, was the fact that they were both transparent—she could see right through them! Their shapes against the dark night sky were like white lines moving on a black background. As they loomed ever larger in front of her, Changel could see stars shining through them.

The mist now covered the ground all around her, from the trees at the far end of the yard to the house. Changel sat frozen in her seat, as the giant and the dog strode toward

her. Then the great dog spotted her and their eyes met. It paused for a moment, gave a great roaring bark—and charged! Its huge black eyes flashed like fire, and saliva dripped from its fierce jaws as it bounded toward her. She could hear it panting, and the sound of its wet feet splashing through the mist. She put her hands over her face, too startled and frightened to scream.

The sound of the dog's breathing became louder and louder until she could hear nothing else. Then she felt the heat of his breath on her hands, and heard a terrible growl. She uncovered her face, ready to scream—and again looked straight into the glowing eyes of the monstrous animal. It had reared up on its hind legs, and was about to pounce on her, when a loud, gruff voice commanded, "Sirius! Hold!"

Changel closed her eyes.

2
Orion

When Changel dared to look again, she saw
the solid legs of the giant standing firmly
behind the black hound. A huge hand with
thick, strong fingers reached down and patted
it on the head. Changel looked slowly up ...
and up ... and up—past the great, laced boots,
the bare knees, the skirt, the animal skin, the
belt, the sword, and the thick arms that now
crossed his chest—all the way up to his long
beard and his face. It was a very long way up.
Wide-eyed, she looked deeply into the black
pools of the giant's eyes. For a long moment
neither of them said a word.

The giant bent his knees and squatted down
beside the dog. "I'm thinking, my faithful
Sirius," he said to the dog, "that this small
creature is not one of the Moon Goddess's

fairies who would do us harm." His great, deep, voice rumbled softly as he ruffled the dog's ears. "Look at her—so frightened that she can hardly move!"

He bent his head close to Changel, and reached over to touch her cheek with his hand. "What's your name, small one?" and asked in a softer voice, "and what are you doing here at a time like this?"

Changel wasn't quite sure what to make of all this. She turned her head and took a quick look at her father, but he was still sound asleep, and it looked as though he was going to stay that way. She looked back at the giant, glad that he had called off his frightening companion. Even now the dog was sniffing at her feet and giving short, friendly wags of its tail.

When she was younger her parents had read her many books about giants and other strange creatures, and they had taken her to see the large animals at the zoo. They had also taught her not to be afraid of the dark, so she was gradually becoming used to this new situation. It was, after all, her own backyard. She made up her mind, and stuck out her chin bravely.

"I'm Changel," she said, with hardly a quiver in her voice, "but who are you? You are too big to come from around here, and so is that dog." She pointed at the animal, being careful not to get her finger too close to its large mouth.

"Ho, ho!" The giant threw back his head and laughed loudly. The dog tried to join in by standing on his hind legs and reaching up to lick the big man's face. Finally they were quiet, and the giant squatted down with his head closer to Changel.

"I am Orion," he said, with eyebrows raised as if surprised at such a silly question. "I seem to have lost my way. This land and all these dwellings are like none I have seen before. Do you know where we are?"

"Where you are?" she answered, with surprise. "This is Pine Valley on Prince Edward Island, and you are in my backyard. That's my father. If you do anything to hurt me, he'll get very angry...."

"Ho, ho!" the giant laughed again. "It isn't your father that I'm worried about, young one with spirit. The Lady Artemis, Diana, is much more likely to cause me grief on this night than any soul in this strange world!"

He paused to look around him. "Strange, indeed," he continued thoughtfully. "There is no such place as Pine Valley or Prince Edward Island in the realms which I frequent. I fear I have taken a wrong turning somewhere—not altogether surprising as we left home somewhat hurriedly and entered paths that I have not trodden in a long time."

"Who are you and why are you in such a hurry?" asked Changel. "And where are you going? Maybe I can help." She had been learning to read road maps lately when the family went for a drive, and she was beginning to think that she could find her way almost anywhere, if she had to—if she had the right map, of course.

"Are you saying that you haven't heard of me, Child? You haven't heard of Orion the Hunter and his faithful companion, Sirius?

Forsooth! It is indeed a new world that we have stumbled into, my old hound," he said, looking from Changel to Sirius.

"Well," continued the strange giant who called himself Orion, "to make a long tale short in the telling, there was once a great King of Chios. He promised me the hand of his daughter in marriage if I would clear his land of wild beasts." At this point, Orion bowed his head for a moment, shaking it a bit from side to side, as if looking back on something that he found hard to believe.

"Oh, yes," he continued. "The king promised me the hand of his beautiful daughter, Merope, but when I had done as he asked and cleared his land of wild beasts, he refused to honor his promise. Instead he betrayed me and gave me poisoned wine while I rested. The wine made me so weak that I could not defend myself. I was forced to flee for my life!

"As I was leaving the palace, I was confronted by the Moon Goddess, who is called either Lady Artemis or Diana. She had wanted to wed me and when she learned that I had been betrothed to another, she became insanely jealous. She said if she could not have me, then no one would." Changel saw a gleam of cold anger come into the giant's eye.

"All is not lost, not by any means," he finished grimly. "I must survive only this one night. If I can be the first to see the dawn, Eos, then my strength will be returned. But Diana, Goddess of the Night, will stop me if she can. Even now she hunts me. Her quiver is full of fiery arrows with which to slay me!

"So I seek the dawn, Child, while fleeing from Diana's wrath. And now I am lost in this strange land with no one but my dog, Sirius, and a girl named Changel to aid me.

"Do you know your way around here?" Orion asked. "Perhaps I could give you a small token of my gratitude if you could show me the way back to familiar paths."

"Well," began Changel, "I do know how to get from here to Lobster Cove, or Charlottetown, or the ferry to Borden...."

"I do not know these places," interrupted Orion, impatiently. "They are of no use to me.

I must get back quickly to my trails in the heavens—in the upper worlds." The mist had cleared and he gestured to the stars and black sky overhead. "I must reach the starpaths that I know, and where I have some allies and friends who will shield me if need be. They will help ease my passage to the dawn."

"Look!" he exclaimed, as he swept his arm in a wide circle around the misty lawn. "There is nothing here that looks like a starpath. I must find one soon, or I have little chance of lasting the night. See there—she shows herself even now over the trees!" He pointed with a broad finger to the top of the spruce grove, where a bright three-quarters moon was just appearing.

"Quickly, Changel." He knelt in front of her and gently placed his wide hands on her shoulders. "Where can I go? Come and show me the path that will lead me back to the skies before her fierce, hot arrows strike me!"

Orion stood up to his full height, lifting Changel from her chair with no more effort than she would need to pick up a toy. He settled her into the crook of his arm and they stood motionless for a moment—the giant tall and still with Changel in his arm, and Sirius leaning against his leg as companion and protector. Orion turned slowly in a circle, holding out his other arm.

"Which way do we go, Changel? Will you help me?"

Recovering from the surprise of being lifted so high off the ground, Changel did some very quick thinking. She wondered if her parents' rule about being careful when talking to strangers applied here. After only a second's thought, she decided that this situation was too unusual for ordinary rules. Talking with a six-metre-tall giant who seemed to want her assistance was hardly the same thing as talking to a stranger on the streets of Charlottetown. And, after all, Orion had stopped the dog from hurting her. Having decided she was safe, or as safe as any person could be in this unusual situation, she turned her attention to Orion's question. Suddenly, she remembered her father's earlier explanation about navigating with the stars. She grabbed Orion's arm with one hand and pointed with the other.

"There might be something I know," she began. "My dad said that if you can find the Big Dipper, and then the North Star, you can figure out everything else from there." She looked up and around.

"There it is!" she exclaimed. "That's the Big Dipper! Yes! If you follow the two stars at the Dipper's base, you can find the North Star, Polaris. See, it's that bright one over there."

Orion scanned the sky in the direction she was pointing and then looked back to where they were standing.

"Yes, I believe you may be right," he said. "It is a somewhat different shape than it should be, but perhaps I am used to seeing it from a different angle. That would explain it. Come, Little One, we have no time to waste. We will go there now, for I already feel the icy eyes of Diana searching for me, and I have no wish to be caught here!"

As he spoke, Orion set off, with great strides, in the direction of the North Star. Changel looked down at his feet swinging through the air. She clutched his arm tightly.

"Wait!" she cried, perhaps a little more loudly than is strictly polite, since she was so close to his ear. "I don't think I really want to go walking in the sky right now, tonight, thank you very much, Mr. Orion."

(Actually, she didn't mind the idea of having an adventure with this strange giant whom she was beginning to like, but she protested automatically. It was like screaming "No," while being pushed off the giant water slide at the amusement park.)

Orion didn't slow down, but kept on taking those great strides, ever higher and higher, heading straight toward the Big Dipper and Polaris.

"What do you mean you don't want to go skywalking?" he thundered, jovially. "It is far and away the quickest and best method of getting anywhere, and you can see so much more than by walking on the surface of a small planet like the one we are leaving behind. I will bring you back safely, before you know it.

I just want to take you along for a while. You have helped me once and I have the feeling you may do so again. Be patient now, for we are almost at the Big Dipper, as you call it. I know it as the Great Bear or Ursa Major. The North Star cannot be far ahead, and that is where I wish to go first."

Changel closed her eyes for a minute until she got used to the idea of "skywalking," as Orion called it. She took a short peek now and then, and saw Pine Valley fading away in the distance. Soon, she could see only the lights of the towns and cities, and then no lights at all except for the million stars around her in the night sky. Orion and Sirius seemed unconcerned as they walked along side by side as if there was a solid path beneath their feet. When they arrived at the North Star Orion stopped to look around.

"You see how sly Diana is," he said to Changel. "She rises in the east at this time, trying to keep me running always toward the west, without ever seeing a sunrise. We will have to ponder how to remove her from that place and put me in it so that this weakness may be lifted from me. I fear I do not have the strength to battle any foes we might encounter."

Changel had become quite used to her new position, and was determined to see as much as possible before the ride ended. The pattern of stars at their feet held her attention.

"Why, it looks as if there are two dippers, Orion!" she exclaimed. "Look—there's the Big Dipper, below us, with stars pointing toward the North Star. But the North Star itself is the end of the handle of a smaller dipper!"

"Why, certainly, Changel," said Orion, "there are two dippers, or Bears—the Greater, or Big Dipper, and the Lesser or Little Dipper. They revolve around one another as the seasons change through the year—that is to say, one of them is always pouring into the other. All stars move in a regular pattern around the sky. So you can find your way around Pine Valley, but not the starpaths, eh?" finished Orion, a twinkle in his eye.

"Well, I did find the Dipper for you, didn't I?" answered Changel, perhaps just a bit huffily. "My dad and I were just starting to look for some others when you showed up. I'll bet I learn to find my way around here pretty soon. By the way, if you're worried about something having to do with the moon, then you'd better have a look behind you!"

Orion looked around, took a step back and drew in his breath. At his feet Sirius growled softly.

Far across the sky, a figure was beginning to float up behind the moon. It was another giant, but this time it was a beautiful woman, with long, flowing hair held back with a golden head band, and wearing a long white gown, fastened at the waist with a jewelled belt. She had a quiver full of arrows slung over one shoulder, and a long bow in one hand. As Changel and Orion watched, she caught sight of them, raised the bow high in a triumphant gesture, and began running across the sky toward them at great speed. As she ran she

reached over her shoulder, drew an arrow from the quiver and notched it to the bow string.

They heard her cry echoing among the stars, "I have you now, Orion!" Her voice was like a North Atlantic gale, screaming furiously, high pitched and bitterly cold. "I have you now, and never shall you see the sun or betray me again!"

Then, Diana (Changel realized this was who it must be), drew the bow to her shoulder and loosed an arrow that flew through the sky like a comet, directly toward the great heart of Orion.

3
On the Run!

As the deadly feathered shaft of the Moon Goddess sped toward them, Orion reacted quickly.

"Come, Sirius!" he commanded. Then still firmly holding Changel, he spun away from Diana, and dropped out of sight behind the Dipper.

As they disappeared over the edge of the skypath behind the Dipper, they heard a scream of cold rage echo across the heavens. Orion paused on this new skypath, looking first in one direction, then the other.

"She is sure to think we are headed for the east, and the coming dawn, so we must go in the opposite direction," he said. "Even if she suspects our plan, she must check the other way first, to make sure we don't get behind her. She knows she will have no vengeance should I find the dawn before her, and renew my strength!"

Orion turned to the west, away from the Dippers, and began to jog along the path. Changel held tightly to his neck with one arm and clung to his garment with her free hand. Sirius ran easily behind them and once, it seemed to Changel, the great black hound turned his head and grinned at her. She gave him a tentative smile. Maybe he wasn't such a fierce dog after all, she thought.

Diana's raging faded into the distance and Orion finally stopped for a rest, breathing deeply. Sirius sat at their feet, tongue lolling to one side of his mouth.

"Where are we, Orion?" asked Changel, "I can't see Pine Valley anymore, or even the Earth! How am I to get home?" A small tear appeared at the corner of her eye.

Orion smiled.

"Do not be afraid, Little One." He spoke

gently. "Although you cannot see your home, it is surely there. It is a little too far away to see right now, but when the time comes for you to return, you may know that each star in these bright heavens will ensure your safe journey."

As Orion spoke, it seemed as if every star in the sky gave a little extra twinkle to tell her it was true. Changel felt reassured and very safe. She gave a little squeeze with the arm that was still around the giant's neck.

"Thank you, Orion," she whispered.

"Ho!" shouted Orion suddenly. "Now I recognize where we are! It has been many long turns of the heavens since I've passed this way, but surely this is the home of the herdsman, Boötes. He must remember me, for I helped him clear his land of the fierce and wild animals, and made it safe for his tame beasts. Yes, surely this is it—for there is the great Northern Crown—the Corona Borealis—which was placed in the sky beside Boötes so long ago. Where is he, now?"

Orion began to look around searching.

"Boötes and the Northern Crown?" Changel

asked. "What do you mean, Orion? Are Boötes and the Northern Crown other constellations like the Dippers?"

"Constellations?" repeated Orion, "Yes, I have heard them called that. In the old tales of Greece and Rome it is told that persons who had done a great service for the gods—or had been tragically killed—were honored by being given a place in the sky. Thus they will be remembered forever."

"I see," said Changel, "so Boötes...."

"There are many stories told about him," explained Orion. "He is sometimes called the Bear Driver—you remember that the stars you called the Big Dipper and Little Dipper are also called the Greater and Lesser Bears?" Changel nodded. "Others call him the Ploughman and the Dippers are his oxen. There are also those who know him as the Hunter and the Dippers become his hunting dogs! You see, Changel, there are different stories from many lands about the stars."

"That's all very well," said Changel, "and I'm sure they are all very interesting, but one version is enough for now. There are an awful lot of stars up here."

"Anyway, about Boötes and the Northern Crown," he continued, "I will tell you briefly what I know while we search for him. When he was young and hot-blooded, he roamed far and wide, hunting wild beasts and seeking adventures through all the world. As he grew older, however, he tired of this sport and became a herdsman, keeping sheep and cattle. But some of the beasts which he used to hunt decided to take their revenge and gathered together against him. I happened to be in the area when they attacked Boötes, and so helped him to drive them off. We have been good acquaintances ever since, although that took place more years ago than I can remember. I have not seen him for a long, long time.

"But we must be close—see, there is the Northern Crown, which I know was placed in the heavens very near to Boötes. The Crown was put there in memory of a beautiful princess whose name was Ariadne. Ariadne helped a brave warrior called Theseus slay the

Minotaur—a fierce creature, half bull and half man. You see, there!" Orion pointed. "There is Ariadne's Crown—the Northern Crown or Corona Borealis—that half circle of seven stars—and there, just beside it—is Boötes! I knew he had to be near. See? Boötes is like a great diamond in the sky, with the bright star Arcturus as the base."

Following Orion's directions it was easy for Changel to locate the Crown and the stars of Boötes. But then the most amazing thing happened—the outline of a huge figure began to appear. He was the size of Orion, but instead of a club and a sword, he held a long shepherd's crook. His hair and beard were shorter and less wild than Orion's, and his face was older and more lined, as if he had spent many years under a hot sun. As he took shape, the giant blinked his eyes, and looked around slowly as if just waking from a long sleep.

"Who then calls for Boötes?" he asked. "Long have I slept—peaceful in my starry sepulchre—for my deeds are well accomplished and my rest well deserved!"

His gaze fell on Orion and Changel.

"You do not belong in this part of the sky," he continued, a frown now appearing on his ancient brow. "Yet I think I recognize you, giant one! Why, it's my old fieldmate Orion, is it not? And that must be your constant companion, Sirius. But who is that you carry in your arms? Come, let me see, old friend. Is this a new addition to our ranks? It has been long since any joined us here. I cannot move without much difficulty these days. Since finally leaving the fields, I am firmly anchored by these stars you see around me—especially by the bright Arcturus. It is a great honor for a simple herdsman."

A broad grin creased Orion's features as he approached Boötes. He transferred Changel to his left arm and held out his right hand to his old comrade. Boötes did likewise, and for a minute they clasped wrists, each gazing affectionately at the other, remembering times long past. Boötes finally broke the silence.

"We must not dally, old friend," he said. "Pleasant though that might be, I do not have long. Soon I will fade again, and be known only by the stars around me. Only the most dire need could have caused my appearance—and your presence tells me that you are the one who needs me. Tell me, Orion, how may I help you?"

"It is a long and distressing tale, Herdsman," answered Orion. "Briefly, I may say that I have been most treacherously used by the King of Chios who has poisoned me. As if this was not bad enough, no sooner had the sickness come upon me, than Diana, who had wished for ages to marry me, discovered that the King's daughter had been promised to me. Diana flew into a jealous rage! My strength will be returned when I again see the dawn, but even now the goddess pursues me with her fiery arrows and would see me dead ere I see the Eos! She is not far behind...." As he spoke, the cry of the Moon Goddess shrieked across the sky.

"I must keep ahead of her or my days are finally done. This child," he added, "has joined me by a strange chance. It would seem that the gods have sent her to help me find my way through this long night."

Boötes looked at Changel thoughtfully, then back to Orion, and frowned.

"I cannot imagine why you have been led this way," he said finally, "for I have little advice or assistance to offer. All I have ..." (here he reached slowly into a pouch at his side) "... are these dull gems which I found longer ago than I can now remember. I have carried them with me always, wondering if they would ever be of use. I do not understand it, but perhaps these are what you need from me," finished Boötes. Three dully shining, diamond-shaped stones now rested in his open palm.

"Boötes," exclaimed Orion, "this is truly amazing!" He set Changel down on the starpath, took the gems from Boötes, holding them lovingly in his great hand.

"I lost these stones when I was but a youth, in one of my first great battles with the bull, Taurus!" Orion gazed far off toward the southern sky as he spoke.

"They were my most treasured possessions, but they were ripped from my belt by the great horns of the beast! We wounded each other grievously that day, and it was long ere I recovered. I had never expected to see them again. Look how they shine, now they that are returned to their rightful place."

Shine they did, as Orion carefully set them into metal fastenings along the front of his wide belt. Immediately he seemed to take on new strength and vitality, and stood a little taller than before, as the bright gems winked and twinkled in the light of a million stars. A fierce grin lit his face for a moment and he turned again to Boötes.

"There is little doubt now why I was led here, or why you felt such a strange compulsion to carry stones you thought worthless for so many eons," he said. "For you see, they give me new hope, new strength, and new will to carry on!"

He laughed joyfully, then turned and to Changel.

"Are they not wondrous, o' small and

beautiful one, shining like the starlight in your eyes?" he asked, smiling widely.

"They are very beautiful, Orion," she answered, "but oh, what is happening to Boötes?"

Just as he had slowly appeared before them minutes before, he was now beginning to fade away.

"Goodbye, old comrade," they heard him say. "It was a great boon to see you one final time! May the gods look favorably upon your quest. Goodbye also to you, Little One! Remember us as we really were!"

Then he was gone.

Orion bent over sadly, and gathered Changel into the crook of his arm. They stood silently for a moment, thinking of the herdsman. But their thoughts were loudly and rudely interrupted by shrill shouts from the direction of the Dippers.

Sirius growled deep in his throat.

Suddenly, a figure appeared on the other side of the Dippers, then leaped to the very top of Polaris, the North Star. It was Diana, her eyes blazing with anger, as she once again raised her bow to the sky, aiming it in their direction.

Changel felt Orion tremble and saw a deep anger welling up in his eyes. He raised his left hand high, and waved his huge club defiantly.

"Were it not for you, Child, I would surely battle her now!" he said angrily. "But, indeed," he added, more softly, "perhaps that is the very purpose for your being here, for I am not yet ready.… "

He took a deep breath.

"Diana!" he shouted, "return to your moon-chariot, and cool your blind anger! I have done you no harm!"

"Never!" screamed Diana, in a voice like thunder. "This dawning is mine, and you shall be punished for your betrayal!"

Diana leaped high above the North Star, landing on the starpath below. Overcome with fury, she paused only long enough to reach into the quiver on her back for another arrow. She quickly fixed it to the bow string, pulled it taut, and then released it with a smooth and practised motion.

This frightful arrow of the Moon Goddess tore a bright gash in the sky, dropping goblets of fire along its glowing path. It flew across the heavens, straight toward the heart of the motionless giant.

With new strength in his legs, Orion turned quickly, and made a great leap away from the flaming arrow. Sirius was close behind. Changel held on tightly as they landed atop the Corona Borealis, the Northern Crown of Ariadne, which Orion quickly put between them and their relentless pursuer.

4
Scorpio

Changel was glad to be out of sight of the fierce goddess, but a loud, angry shriek reminded her that Diana was still on their trail. Even Sirius was glancing back with a worried look in his great eyes.

"Orion," ventured Changel, as they ran along the path, "I still don't understand why she hates you so."

Lines of worry furrowed his great brow, but he smiled and gently ruffled her hair.

"She's not really as bad as she sounds, Changel," he said, "but she is very hot-tempered, and very spoiled and used to having her own way—and very, very dangerous when she gets like this! She has long said that she loved me and would have me for her husband, but I never agreed to marriage. I had been too busy to think of a bride until I fell in love with Merope, and made the agreement with her father. Diana felt she had been betrayed, although she really had no reason. Once the night passes and a new day comes, she will realize that what she now sees as a terrible outrage was not intended to hurt her. Sometimes even big-hearted people can be bad-tempered and unreasonable if they don't get their way, and may do things they will later regret. I certainly hope that you don't lose your temper as easily as Diana does!"

"Oh, I don't think so!" said Changel seriously. "It doesn't seem like a very nice way to be."

"It certainly isn't!" agreed Orion. "Still we had better keep out of her reach."

Orion paused momentarily to look around. Then he began to run, keeping the Northern Crown between them and Diana. "I may have thought of a way to get past her, if we can just get to the Swan," he explained to Changel as he ran.

"Look there, now—isn't that Hercules?" he

asked, pointing to some stars in the distance as they ran on. Changel watched, and sure enough there briefly appeared the outline of another giant. This one was kneeling on one knee, with a club in one hand and what looked like a branch in the other.

"Hercules?" asked Changel, "I think I've heard of him. Wasn't he a great fighter, Orion?"

"Something like that, Young One," answered Orion. "He is famous for the Twelve Labours of Hercules—twelve tasks which were so difficult that no one could complete them until he came along. He was very strong, which is what he is best remembered for, but he also did some things which made him many enemies. No one knows for sure, but this is perhaps why he has been placed in the sky in that kneeling position, to appease some of the gods whom he angered in life.

"And over there," he continued, pointing beyond Hercules, "is the great Lyre of Orpheus! What would the heavens be without music? That is perhaps the most famous instrument, which made the most beautiful sounds ever known. It was fashioned by the god Mercury from a great tortoise shell, and given to Orpheus, who cast a spell over gods and mortals alike with his enchanting music. The Lyre was placed in the sky when he died, so none would forget him. Some say it was placed near Hercules to help him find peace. It does contain one of the most beautiful stars—Vega."

Changel watched with awe, as the giant lyre, shaped something like a harp, appeared in the sky around the large, bright star called Vega. It seemed as if a giant hand also appeared, and strummed the Lyre, just once.

"For now, we must not delay. Though it seems contrary to our purpose we must head west. We may face more danger, perhaps, for somewhere not far ahead is Sagittarius, the Archer—comrade, these many years, of Diana. We must...."

But Changel heard no more, for Orion's voice was silenced by a blinding flash as a huge star fell out of the sky toward them.

Changel screamed ... Sirius barked ... and Orion roared. Fortunately for all of them, as he yelled, Orion grabbed Sirius's collar and jumped backward. The huge fireball crashed onto the starpath where they had been standing, and they heard a great laugh from far away.

"You cannot avoid the Archer, Orion!" cried a voice, "For if you do not come to me, I can shoot the stars themselves out of the sky and drop them where I choose."

Off in the distance, where the laughter continued, they saw the Archer. He was unlike anyone Changel had seen before. He had the body of a huge horse, with the chest, arms and head of a man. His head was thrown back in laughter, with his hair streaming out behind. He reared on his hind legs as they watched, and reached for another arrow in a quiver which hung from his shoulder.

At that very moment Orion made a tremendous leap to one side and they landed, breathless, on another path which ran steeply down hill—a hill covered with ice! They slid down the great dome of the sky, leaving the laughing Archer and the pursuing Diana far behind. Changel, enjoying the gigantic slide and determined to make the most of this adventure, thought that perhaps now their troubles were over. Orion's grim look, however, quickly dashed her hopes.

"I fear we have fallen into a clever trap, Little One," he said. "Whether it is an intentional trap or simply bad luck, we are in great danger. Unless I am very much mistaken, we are being carried down into the lair of one of the most fearsome creatures in the entire sky—a creature which even I was unable to defeat. It was given a special purpose by an ancient king whom I once battled long ago— and that purpose is to cause my death!"

Changel tightened her grip on Orion's neck, and on Sirius, who was sliding along beside them.

"My goodness," she said, not without a little touch of exasperation in her voice, "there are certainly a lot of unpleasant people and creatures up here. Who could possibly be worse than that horseman or the moon person? It must be very bad to...."

Before she could *say* how bad it must be, she *saw* instead how bad it was. For facing them was the most ghastly creature imaginable. Changel recognized it from pictures in her school science books, but the scorpions she remembered were very small. This one was monstrous—at least as long as Orion was tall and, even crouched on all six legs, it came up to Orion's belt. The creature raised its long tail and rattled its scales, as the three travellers thumped to a stop at the bottom of the slope. Sirius, his teeth bared, laid back his ears and began barking furiously. Orion quickly set Changel down and stepped in front of her.

"At last, Orion, we meet again." hissed the scorpion. "You escaped me once before when I should have ended your days. Now there is no escape from my lair—except by death!"

It waved its claws, and drew back its tail ready to fling it forward toward its victim. Changel screamed. Orion did the only thing possible to counter the attack and protect Changel. He raised his sword high with both hands, as if to smash it down on the scorpion's

head, and rushed boldly toward the monster, right between the waving claws.

Scorpio, for that was the creature's name, stopped for a moment in confusion, not expecting a direct attack. Then it turned sideways to avoid Orion's sword, and at the same time snapped its deadly sting over its head in a stabbing motion. Orion jumped to one side, narrowly avoiding being grabbed by one of the great claws, and lashed out in a powerful two-handed slash with his sword. The sword dug into one of the scorpion's front legs. It screamed and lurched, almost falling. Orion circled around to the side of its injured leg so that the creature had to turn to protect itself. Changel was now out of immediate danger.

The combatants sparred back and forth. The scorpion rushed Orion as best as it could with its injured leg, while Orion avoided the waving claws and tail and tried to land a fatal blow to its head. Sirius circled around, barking and growling while looking for an opening. Finally he found one. He dashed in and fastened his thick, strong jaws around one of the scorpion's rear legs. Scorpio, roaring in pain and anger, turned instinctively to meet this new attack. It was the opening that Orion needed. In an instant he leaped through the scorpion's defences, and thrust his sword deeply between its eyes, dealing it a mortal wound.

The scorpion gave a great death scream, raised its head and reared back on its hind legs. Sirius let go and leaped out of the way of its thrashing claws and stinger. As the great Scorpio fell, its fearsome tail whipped toward Changel. Orion saw what was about to happen and, with a loud cry of dismay, leaped to protect her. Wielding his great sword he managed to catch the deadly stinger with the thick blade. There was a loud, sharp crack as sword and stinger met. Then the scorpion lay still—dead at last.

Orion, stunned by the power released in his final blow, fell back onto the ice hill beside Changel. Changel stared at him in dismay, fearful that he might be injured. Sirius, also concerned, leaped up beside Orion and began licking his face, once even laying the great tongue hastily across Changel's nose. (It was so big it actually covered her whole face.) After a few seconds of this treatment, Orion came round sputtering and laughing.

"Enough, Sirius, enough!" he laughed. "I'm all right. How is everyone else?" he hugged Sirius with one great arm and Changel with the other.

"You were right—it was worse than the moon-person or the horseman," said Changel, staring wide-eyed at the dead scorpion. "But look—what has happened to your sword?"

Orion's sword lay in front of them, still smoking and pulsating from that last great blow. But now, welded into the metal of the blade, were three gems, bright and shining like diamonds. Gently picking up the sword, like a man handling something very precious, Orion examined it closely.

Changel reached over to touch it. Her small hand barely covered one of the sparkling jewels.

"Oh," she said, softly, "the middle one is full

of light, like swirling clouds...." She raised her face to the stars shining above the bowl-like depression of the scorpion's lair.

"It is! It's just like the stars up there above us, only in the sword it's as if we were looking through a window at the universe. It's as if we were here, and also there...."

Orion smiled at Changel.

"You see a great deal from those young eyes, don't you, Little One?"

His eyes scanned the heavens, as Changel's had done, but only for a second. Then his muscles tightened, as he breathed in sharply and jumped to his feet. Changel realized immediately what was wrong.

Diana stood at the top of the ice hill, near the spot where the fireball had crashed. Her eyes were black and cold and wild with anger.

"So, Hunter," she cried, "you have escaped once again from the death you so deserve. You must fall soon, and then I will have you. But I would sooner take you now!"

Diana braced herself on the slope of the ice hill and pulled another arrow from her quiver to fix to her bow. Orion and Changel realized they were trapped in the scorpion's lair. Orion looked around desperately but could see no way out.

"So, I must face that terrible bow at last," he said. "Weakened as I am, I have little chance against her. But wait—perhaps there is one small hope."

In one stride he was beside the scorpion, where it lay with its tail curled over its back. Quickly he grabbed Changel, and seated himself astride the end of the dead creature's tail.

"Come, Sirius, old fellow!" he shouted to the dog, indicating a place beside him. "It's all right!"

Sirius leaped up and settled himself, while Orion firmly grasped both the dog and the little girl with one strong arm.

"Let's hope this works," he said. "Even now, the sting of the scorpion may contain enough power in the muscles for one last contraction. If I can just find the right nerve to release it...."

Strangely enough, in this moment of great

danger, Changel remembered a science program she had seen on TV, explaining how the muscles of animals worked. Sometimes, she recalled, energy trapped in the muscles could be released, allowing short bursts of movement after an animal had died. She watched Orion's stabbings with interest.

Carefully he poked his sword into the joint of the huge tail, but nothing happened. Diana was also watching. Realizing what Orion was attempting, she screamed angrily and began sliding down the ice hill toward them. Suddenly Orion's prodding sword struck the right nerve, and the great scorpion tail straightened out like a giant catapult.

Changel, Orion and Sirius flew off wildly into the night sky, right over the screaming Diana's head. They left her behind as the long, flaming arrow that she shot at them fell hopelessly short.

5
Pegasus, the Winged Horse

"Oh … *ah!*" cried Changel with a mixture of fear and excitement, as they flew across the sky, holding each other tightly. It wasn't really all that scary, considering some of the things they had already been through. Changel thought this could be lots of fun were it not for the fearsome person behind them with her terrible bow and flaming arrows. Sirius's big, black face was right beside her, and she felt his breath like warm laughter on her cheek. Orion chuckled softly behind her.

"It's about time we had a little luck," he said. "The tail has flung us more or less in an easterly direction, which is precisely where we need to go. Diana will have a hard time catching up to us now, I think."

They were high above the starpath they had walked along before, and Changel could see everywhere—above and below, and off to each side, as well as in front. She had never realized there were so many stars.

"Orion," she began.

"Yes, Little One?" he replied.

"I know I keep asking this, but where are we? And since there are no star maps, like the road maps we have on Earth, how do you know where we are?"

"Where are we?" repeated Orion, as they gradually slowed down and came to rest on another starpath. "Why, we are high in the sky that you see at night from your Earth, which is far below us—much too far away to see. Imagine your home is a little dot down there, with a huge bowl covering it. While you were standing on Earth you looked up into the bowl. Now you're standing way up on top of the bowl and the stars are all around us. When you are up here, you can see that it's not just one bowl, but many bowls, each one bigger than the one under it.

Changel nodded to let him know she understood.

"For me to tell you exactly where we are, you would have to know a little bit about how to find your way around up here. You would need some kind of map."

"Like a road map, of course," said Changel, "We need a road map of the stars."

"Well, then," continued Orion, "first come up here where you can see better." He lifted her from between his feet where she had seated herself beside Sirius, and onto his huge knee.

"There, that's better. I was lost when I found myself in Pine Valley," he said, "because I was more used to seeing things from up here. Now that I'm back in familiar surroundings, I can see all the old landmarks."

"Yes, of course," Changel agreed. "It's like the watertower in Pine Valley or a church steeple, which you can see from far away. It lets you know where you are."

"Yes, that's it exactly," answered Orion. "For me the patterns of stars which make up the many constellations in the sky are my

landmarks. The Big Dipper or Bear, and the North Star, for instance, are two of the easiest places to recognize. From there, as you now know, you can find almost everything else— the Northern Crown of the Princess Ariadne, or the Herdsman Boötes. Further to the west, from where we have just escaped, are the stars of Sagittarius, the Archer, who shot the star onto our path. And over there are the stars which make up the terrible Scorpion. Can you see the triangle forming his body, and the tail?"

Changel, who had listened to Orion's descriptions with great interest, began to see the pattern of the stars all around her.

"Now," Orion continued, "that huge white band of millions and millions of stars below us is called the Milky Way, because the stars are so thick that it looks as if someone had spilled a giant glass of milk all across the sky. Even in the Milky Way there are other groups of stars you can recognize. Here is Cassiopeia, with five stars that look like the letter W on its side. Cassiopeia was once a beautiful Queen, and now she rests in the sky to watch over her daughter, Andromeda."

Although Changel concentrated as hard as she could, she found it a little difficult to take it all in.

"There are so many of them!" she cried in exasperation. "How do you learn them all?"

"Why," answered Orion, with a little laugh, "just the way you learn everything else—one step at a time. Sometimes it helps to have an adventure so that you get to know the characters and their stories first hand. Then when you look around the sky, you will recognize the different characters, like landmarks on a map. There, toward the east, where we are going—past Cassiopeia and Andromeda—can you see the four stars which make a great square?"

Changel followed his pointing finger.

"Yes," she said.

"Look a little harder."

Changel concentrated on the four stars which made up the square—and suddenly they became the outline of a huge horse taking shape. It was the most amazing horse she had ever seen—for it had wings. As it gradually appeared it looked to be in full stride, galloping joyously across the skies, long front legs reaching, hind legs bent as if ready to leap right out of the heavens. Its wings were stretched to their fullest, and the great head was held high and proud, the mane streaming behind. It was the most wonderful creature Changel had ever seen.

"Oh!" was all she could think of saying.

Orion raised his head, and cupped his hands around his mouth.

"Pegasus!" he yelled, and waved an arm high overhead in greeting.

Pegasus, the winged horse, turned to see who had hailed him. When he saw Orion he whinnied loudly and reared even higher in a joyous greeting. He took a great jump, and landed beneath them. They climbed onto his back, between the huge wings. Changel could not help herself—she reached out and hugged the white neck, as they flew back to the four stars which marked Pegasus's place in the sky.

"Whatever has caused you and your faithful Sirius to come flying across the sky like some great birds, mighty Hunter?" asked Pegasus, as they came to rest. "And who is your small but delightful companion? I had thought that your adventures were completed!"

"Oh, it is a long and terrible story, winged Pegasus," replied Orion, "but I will try to make it short, as our time here is also short."

Then Orion told Pegasus of the adventures he and Sirius had shared with Changel.

"Now," he concluded, "I hope that all will be well, for the dawn is not far off. When I reach the sun my powers will be restored, and Diana will no longer be a threat to me. Look— even now I see the first light in the eastern sky!"

While Orion and Pegasus talked Changel lovingly stroked the great horse's mane and neck, and looked wonderingly at the huge, powerful wings. Sirius jumped down and lay at the feet of Pegasus, panting contentedly like any ordinary dog. Suddenly, his ears perked up. He got to his feet quickly and looked back along the Milky Way, which they had so recently crossed. A low growl escaped from his throat.

"How long did you say until the dawn, Hunter?" Pegasus asked quietly.

"A very short time now," replied Orion. "Why do you ask?"

"A very short time may be too long, I am afraid," said Pegasus softly. "Look toward the Milky Way."

Orion saw her first, and his lips tightened in anger and dismay. There was Diana, who had escaped the lair of Scorpio much faster than he expected. She was running rapidly along the bright starpath, her head turning from side to side as she searched for them. While they watched, her eyes found the square of Pegasus. She shouted loudly in triumph, and waved one hand above her head while the other clenched her bow. She screamed at them triumphantly.

"This time there is nowhere left to hide, Orion! I have you now, and you will never see the dawn!"

Once again she notched an arrow to her bowstring and dashed toward them like a flaming comet in the sky. It was apparent, even to Changel, that if they tried to run to the east, Diana would cut them off long before they reached the brightening horizon.

Changel looked from Orion to Pegasus, not understanding.

"It's not so bad, is it, Orion?" she asked. "Can't the great, winged horse take us to the dawn, or anywhere else for that matter, and outrun the Moon Goddess?"

"Ah, I am afraid not, Child," answered Orion, patting her shoulder gently and rubbing Pegasus's white side, as he spoke. "Pegasus, you see, is like Boötes—he is attached to these stars and can move only a very short distance away from them."

"That is true," confirmed Pegasus. "But I may be able to be of some assistance anyway. If you run now to my other side before she gets here, so that she has to go around behind me to follow you, I just might have a small surprise for her."

Orion paused for a second, trying to discover the meaning of the smile lighting the horse's eyes. But there was no time to ask questions, for Diana was drawing ever closer. Orion made up his mind quickly.

"Pegasus is right, Changel," he said. "We have little choice. I hate to leave, when we are so very close, but we must. Come!"

He placed Changel in the crook of his arm once again, put his other arm around Pegasus's neck, and hugged him.

"You know my gratitude is too great for words, trusted and faithful friend," he said, laying his cheek against the cheek of the white horse. "Come, Sirius! Away!"

Then he dashed around behind Pegasus, with Sirius close behind. They heard Diana's laughter behind them. She was much closer than Changel had realized—much too close.

It's over, Orion!" Diana shouted, her voice sounding so clear that she might leap upon them any second.

Suddenly Orion cried out in pain, stumbled and almost fell. Sirius barked, as Orion halted quickly and set Changel on the path. Her eyes fell on the barbed and flaming arrow lodged in Orion's heel.

"Oh, no!" she cried, in dismay.

She was sure that this attack was the end of the chase. Diana triumphantly waved her bow and ran behind Pegasus to catch them at last. But then, taking them all by surprise, the two huge hind legs of Pegasus lashed out at her. The great hooves struck Diana squarely and, screaming with surprise, arms spread wide, she flew backwards through the sky, back toward the Milky Way—away and away and away.

The three comrades watched in disbelief.

"Hurry!" shouted Pegasus, "That will delay her a bit, but it's the only chance you'll get. Run, Orion, run!"

Orion grimaced in pain, bent down and yanked the arrow from his foot. Taking Changel in his arms, he set off down the starpath, with Sirius close beside him.

6
Cygnus, the Swan

This time it seemed to Changel they ran on endlessly. On and on—and always away from the dawn which was so important to Orion. On and on, with faithful Sirius bounding beside them. Changel knew that Orion was hurting from the wound in his foot—he limped with every step, often stumbling and nearly losing his balance. There was pain in his eyes and his breathing was heavy. But on they ran.

Orion called out the names of the constellations as they passed and spoke of them all fondly, as if they were old friends or acquaintances.

There was the constellation called Pisces, the Fish. Orion told Changel the story of Venus and Cupid, who were chased by an evil giant, and finally had to leap into a river and change themselves into fish to escape. There was Leo, the Lion, which was killed by Hercules as one of his twelve labours. The Lion was placed in the sky because it had fought such an heroic battle.

There was Cancer, the Crab, also slain by Hercules, and Gemini, the Twins who were also great warriors.

Orion also pointed out some of the planets— planets which were named for ancient gods or goddesses: the red planet Mars, named for the god of war, and the yellowish planet Venus, named for the goddess of love.

Finally, when it seemed as if they had been running forever, Orion slowed to a walk, stopped and sat down. He looked back along the path they had travelled. "I do not think she follows us any longer. I have heard nothing for a long time, and there is no other sign of her."

"Well," answered Changel, "that's good news, isn't it?"

"I don't know," said Orion. "It may mean

that she has decided to give up the chase, since it is nearly dawn and I must be in the east to greet it or all is lost. If Diana is guarding all the approaches to the east, then she knows I have no choice but to confront her sooner or later."

"Orion," said Changel, frowning, "why do you have to go to the east? Won't the dawn come here just like everywhere else if we wait for it?"

"Of course it will, Little One," answered Orion, smiling, "but that is not the point. For if Diana greets the dawn before I do, on this one night only, then she will have won her victory just as surely as if she had put her last arrow in my heart instead of my heel. If Diana greets the dawn, then she will take from it either by persuasion or with her bow, the power I need to regain my strength. Then all is lost for me. The first rays of the morning sun, and the first rays only, are a special life-giver to the first person who tastes them. If that person is to be me, then hiding here will avail me nothing!"

Orion now sat deep in thought.

"There is only one way that I can think of going," he said to Changel. "It is very risky, but I have no other choice. Will you share this final attempt with me, Changel, or shall I have faithful Sirius return you now to your home in Pine Valley? I do not know what your role is in all this, if indeed you have one, but I do think that this will be a risky path."

Changel didn't have to think twice. "I'm coming with you, of course. I'm not quitting now."

A smile pulled at the corner of Orion's bearded mouth as he lifted Changel to his shoulder. He explained the plan as they trotted along.

"We must pass again behind the Herdsman and the Dippers, and approach the long Milky Way from far down in the sky," he said to Changel. "Then we will run up as fast as we can along the Milky Way, and hope that Diana has indeed remained in the east. If we can get high enough above her, then perhaps—just perhaps—we will see the morning sun before she realizes our intention. It is not a great plan, but I am afraid I can think of no other."

"It seems like a very good plan to me, Orion," said Changel, in her most positive voice.

It worked well, even better than they had hoped—for a time.

As they passed the Dippers and approached the great, star-filled Milky Way, they felt a rushing wind around them, and heard a voice speaking from somewhere above their heads.

"Orion," said a voice that was soft and gentle, yet deep. "Orion, why are you racing around the heavens like a fugitive? You are the courageous hero of countless legends, the greatest hunter of all, the victor in many battles, the slayer of great beasts. Who could have wounded you and made you flee? What is the meaning of this?"

The voice seemed to surround them. Although Changel had been sure that after Pegasus nothing could surprise her, she found she had been mistaken. Above them, flying along the Milky Way, was another amazing star-creature—this time a huge bird, white and long-necked—a swan! Its wings were spread wide, and it stretched its long neck as it turned its head toward them. It was outlined by four large bright stars—one at each wing tip, one at its head and one at its feet.

"Cygnus!" exclaimed Orion, looking overhead, "my old companion, Cygnus, the Swan. I had hoped to find you here. You would not believe who has me chasing around the skies. It is Diana, the Huntress, who is pursuing me as I try to reach the dawn. My ordeal has been terrible, but at least it has brought me a new companion—and a greater understanding of mortals, of which she is one, and a very special one. Her name is Changel. She is from the Earth planet. She is sharp-eyed and fearless. Without her help I doubt I would have made it through this night."

Changel continued to gaze in disbelief at the huge swan. She pulled at Orion's robe with her free hand to get his attention. "Who is that?" she whispered.

"Ah, Changel," he answered, with a new lightness in his voice. "I keep forgetting that you do not know all my old comrades. This is

Cygnus, the Swan, who guards the Milky Way to the north, flying endlessly above, always to the north and never reaching it. Cygnus was once a great god who desired to marry a fair mortal, Leda. Leda, however, was already wed to a powerful king. The god turned himself into a beautiful swan to try to lure Leda away, but he was found out and banished forever to this eternal home in the sky, always to seek and never to find. I had hoped we might meet him, for he may be able to help us."

Orion approached Cygnus—who was watching them closely, especially Changel. He reached out his great long neck and wrapped a huge wing protectively around them.

"I will be only too glad to do what I can," said Cygnus, "for you and the little one you bring with you. She has indeed a great spirit, as I can already tell."

As he spoke, Cygnus tried to edge his head between Orion and Changel. Orion pushed him away firmly and laughed.

"That is good, great Swan, and as helpful as I had hoped," he said. "But you must not try

to keep the child with you—as if she, or anyone, could take the place of your lost Leda. Changel must be returned to her home when this night and our adventure are ended, whichever way it may come out. It is not for you or me to keep her here—as you well know."

The Swan pulled back its head, sadly.

"You are right, Orion," Cygnus said wistfully. "She would have been a welcome companion for me—someone to talk to during my lonely days. But she must be returned to her rightful home."

"Of course, Cygnus," replied Orion, "Come now, old friend, if you are to assist me, we must away!"

He climbed onto the Swan's broad back, just behind the neck, reached for Changel and called to Sirius.

"Come, Cygnus, you great winged beast!" he shouted, "Fly us high over the Milky Way, so that we can find the dawn!"

The huge bird served them as well as any friend could, carrying them high above the Milky Way and far into the center of the sky.

As he flew, Orion told him of the night's adventures and what he now hoped to accomplish. Finally, Cygnus slowed, then stopped.

"I am afraid that this is as far as I can go, Orion," he said, "for even now I feel the pull of my stars and must return to my place in the sky."

He lowered his neck gently so that the three companions could slide down onto the starpath. Then, as they watched, Cygnus faded from sight, swiftly winging his way toward the northern path from which he had just carried them. He called to them softly, as he faded away, "Goodbye and good luck. Let no harm come to the child—I shall be watching."

They waved and called farewell until he had gone. In the very short time that she had spent with him, Changel had come to love the huge swan with the sad heart and eyes, just as she had come to love the great winged horse. She waved until all she could see was the four stars in the shape of a cross. Orion lifted Changel into his arms.

"It is good, I think," he said. "We are far above the normal plane of the sky where Diana would expect to see us. Even now, we are slowly drifting down toward the Milky Way. I can see the light at the eastern horizon which means the dawn is about to come. Now we must walk a little farther in that direction until the night is gone. There has been no sign of Diana. We...."

But Orion's words died on his lips. For there, directly between the three companions and the growing light, rising just ahead of the dawn, like a huge, evil statue, was the Moon Goddess herself—Diana. She grinned a terrible, triumphant smile as she slowly and deliberately drew a fiery shaft from her quiver and placed it to her bow. Then, with the speed of the moonbeam which she rode, she flew at them over the sky.

Sirius barked and leaped in apprehension.

"Run, Orion!" screamed Changel. "Run, run, run!"

7
Diana's Revenge

Orion raised his fist in anger, turned to the south, and began to run. Sirius bounded along at his side. Orion's wounded heel slowed him, and Diana laughed in exultation as she rapidly gained on them. Toward the east, they heard a whinny of anger and despair from the winged horse, Pegasus. It seemed that there was no place left for them to run or hide.

Changel glanced behind and saw a sight she would never forget. Diana stood in all her angry splendor, high above them—feet spread apart, head thrown back, and eyes flashing. Then she slowly brought her bow up from her side, a terrible burning arrow already notched and ready to fly.

The edge of the sun gradually began to show above the horizon.

"Look, Orion! Look to the east! The sun is coming up! It's coming. Look, look!"

Orion turned as the rays of the sun streaked across the sky toward them, dancing and glittering among the stars, throwing back the night. Orion stretched out his hand—just one touch, one touch was all he needed.

But just before the first sunbeam reached his grasping fingers, Diana's flaming arrow overtook it. The sizzling arrow pierced Orion's outstretched palm. He howled in agony as the glowing tip nailed his hand to the starry backdrop of the sky. Changel, unable to look, slid from his arm and fell to her knees beside Sirius. Diana, standing triumphantly above them, pulled another blazing shaft from her quiver. With his good hand, Orion reached desperately for his mighty sword. The three stars on his belt and the three on the sword-blade flashed brightly, but he never drew the sword, for Diana's second shaft struck him in the shoulder. Orion cried out again in pain. Sirius howled in anguish, and Changel threw her arms around the great dog's neck.

Tears streamed down Changel's face as she saw Diana draw her final arrow. The Moon Goddess was no longer smiling—she looked grim, perhaps even sorrowful. But still determined to finish what she had started, she drew the great bow one last time and loosed the final shaft. It sped straight and true, and pierced Orion in the centre of his huge chest. This time the arrow went straight through him, picking up speed, as if given a new burst of energy from his great heart, and blazed like a comet across the morning sky.

While Changel watched in horror and disbelief, Orion began to fade from sight just as Boötes and Pegasus and Cygnus had done. Just before he faded completely, his face become peaceful and a tear glistened in the corner of his eye.

"Well, Little One, it's been a grand night, don't you think?" he whispered. "I'm so very glad I met you. What an adventure we have had."

Then he was gone, leaving only the stars— the ones that marked the spots where Diana's arrows had pierced his hand and shoulder, the three stars on his belt, the three on his sword, and two others, which now marked his legs.

Changel realized that Sirius too was fading away. There was a huge bright star beginning to shine at the tip of his nose. But just as the star emerged, the big black dog that she had come to love and trust reached down and gave her a big slurp across her face. Then he was gone.

Changel looked up tearfully at Diana. The Moon Goddess was not laughing any more—she was on her knees, weeping. Her voice, which just a moment ago was shrill and angry, was now sad and gentle. "Oh, my great love, I'm sorry, I'm so sorry," she cried. "You shall blaze forever in my heart ... eternally in the wintry night."

Changel was puzzled. Why did the Moon Goddess who had pursued Orion so relentlessly seem so sad now that she had caught him? How could you love someone and then destroy him?

The sun was directly above the horizon now, and its bright rays encircled Changel. She put her hands to her face and closed her eyes....

"Angel! Angel! Wake up, wake up!" A distant voice called to her. She opened her eyes, but could see nothing for a moment. There was her father, kneeling beside her lawn chair, his hands gently shaking her shoulders.

"My goodness, whatever were you dreaming about?" he asked, smiling. "I've never heard anything so sad in my life—big tears and the saddest, saddest cry."

Eyes wide, Changel studied his face carefully. She reached out and touched his cheek and glasses.

"Oh, Dad," she said finally, throwing her arms around his neck and hugging him as if she'd never let go. He picked her up in his arms, then gathered up the star book and flashlight.

"I guess you fell asleep for a bit, eh?" he said. "It's time for bed. Mom is going to wonder what has happened to us."

He took a last look around the night sky. A mist was beginning to form around the base of the spruce grove and to roll across the lawn toward them.

"It has been a good night," he continued. "I think we've learned something. There's the Big Dipper, and Polaris. Let's see...."

"And over there," Changel said suddenly, pointing. "Look, there's Orion. Can you see his hand and shoulder and the three stars in his belt and in his sword? And there's faithful Sirius beside him."

A puzzled expression crossed her father's face. He remembered the picture of Orion in the star book. He looked at the constellation, then at Changel.

Her eyes were closed. He didn't want to wake her, so he decided to save his questions for the morning. As he turned toward the house, Changel half-opened her eyes and looked over his shoulder.

Far away in the starry night sky, the Great Hunter, Orion, tossed his head and laughed merrily. He waved a wave that only Changel could see and beside him, faithful to the very end, the great black hound Sirius raised his head and woofed a woof that only she could hear.

Changel smiled a secret smile, and in her mind, she waved back to them. Then she shut her eyes and nestled deeper in her father's arms as he crossed the lawn to the house.